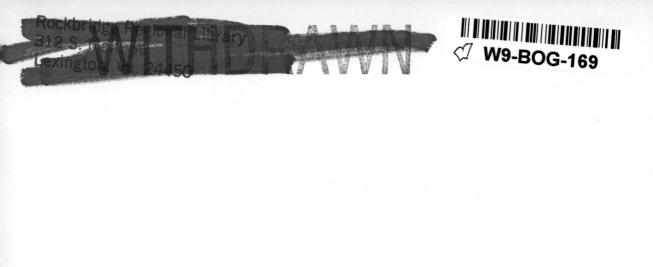

An Early Career Book

careers at a
ZOO

Mark Lerner

photographs by
Milton J. Blumenfeld

Lerner Publications Company
Minneapolis, Minnesota

To Tyrone

LIBRARY OF CONGRESS CATALOGING IN PUBLICATION DATA

Lerner, Mark.
  Careers at a zoo.

  (An Early Career Book)
  SUMMARY: Describes 15 careers at a zoo, including zoo
keeper, veterinarian, animal commissary keeper, graphic arts
specialist, zoo stores supervisor, and the director of visitor
programs.

  1. Zoological gardens—Vocational guidance—Juvenile literature. 2. Zoology—Vocational guidance—Juvenile literature.
[1. Zoological gardens—Vocational guidance. 2. Zoology—
Vocational guidance. 3. Occupations] I. Blumenfeld, Milton J.
II. Title.

QL50.5.L47 1980   590'.74   80-19614
ISBN 0-8225-0342-5   (lib. bdg.)

International Standard Book Number: 0-8225-0342-5 Library of Congress Catalog Card Number: 80-19614

1 2 3 4 5 6 7 8 9 10 85 84 83 82 81 80

Would you like to work at a zoo?

The zoo is a special place where people can see animals from all over the world. In one afternoon, they may see tigers from India, lions from Africa, and polar bears from Alaska. At the zoo, people can also learn about animals. They can find out what a whale eats and where a monkey sleeps. The zoo helps people to understand that animals are an important and exciting part of our world.

Many people work at the zoo. Some of the workers help to make the zoo a comfortable and healthy home for the animals. Others help visitors to enjoy their day at the zoo. No matter what their jobs are, all of the zoo workers try their best to make the zoo the special place that it is.

ZOO KEEPER

Zoo keepers work with animals. They feed the animals and keep their living quarters clean. They also watch the animals very closely to make sure they are healthy. If an animal is behaving in an unusual way or is not eating right, a zoo keeper sees that it is checked. Keepers also must know when the female animals are ready to have babies so they can receive special care.

Zoo keepers often work with only certain kinds of animals. Some keepers take care of reptiles such as snakes and frogs. Other keepers take care of birds. Still others take care of mammals such as tigers and lions. Zoo keepers get to know and care for their animals just as you would care for your own pet dog or cat.

CURATOR

Curators *supervise*, or instruct, the zoo keepers. They decide what the zoo keepers should feed the animals. Like zoo keepers, curators must know a lot about animals. They must also be able to tell when an animal is sick or injured. Curators learn their jobs by working with animals for many years. Many of them were keepers before they became curators.

Curators also design *environments*, or the living quarters or surroundings, for the animals. They know that animals such as bats must have dark environments and that other animals such as beavers must have an environment with water. Curators want to be sure an animal's zoo home is as much as possible like the surroundings the animal had before it came to the zoo.

EXHIBIT CURATOR

Exhibit curators build the homes for the animals that have been designed by the curators. These homes are called *exhibits*. Exhibit curators try to build exhibits to look as much as possible like the animals' natural homes. They also want to build exhibits that are easy to clean and that make it easy for visitors to see the animals.

Exhibit curators use materials such as cement, paint, fiberglass, and plaster to make trees, rocks, caves, and other objects for the exhibits. Exhibit curators are very good at making these objects look real.

Can you guess what the exhibit curator in this picture is painting? He is painting a plastic coral reef for the tropical fish aquarium. It looks like the coral that was in the fishes' ocean home.

VETERINARIAN

Veterinarians are the zoo's doctors. They take care of the zoo's sick and injured animals. Veterinarians also *vaccinate* (VAK-sin-nate) the animals so the animals will not catch certain diseases.

Veterinarians have trained for many years in schools of veterinary medicine and know animals as well as medical doctors know people. Some veterinarians take care of only one kind of animal, but zoo veterinarians treat all kinds of animals — from alligators to zebras.

The veterinarian in the picture is treating an injured ram. He and his assistant, an animal health specialist, have shaved the wool off one of the ram's back legs. Now they will put the leg into a cast so it can heal.

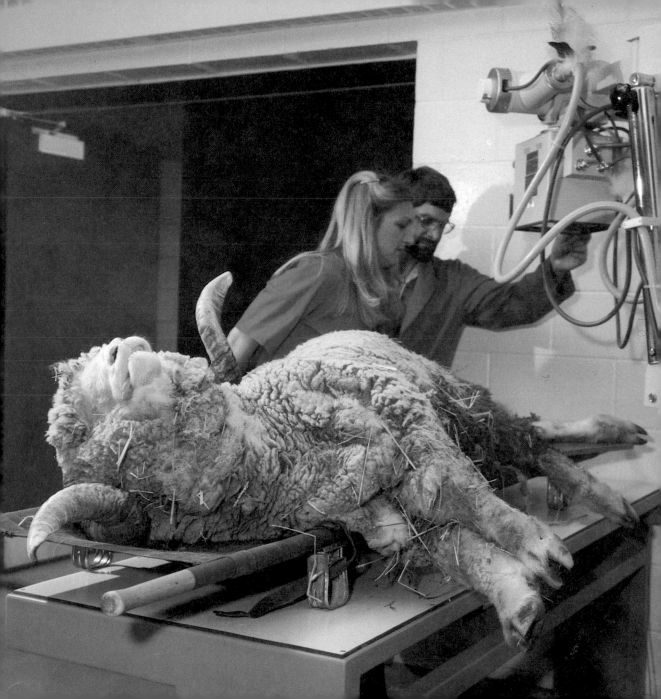

HORTICULTURIST

Horticulturists take care of all of the zoo's plants. They grow them in the zoo greenhouse and later plant them in the exhibits. When plants get sick, horticulturists nurse them back to health.

Horticulturists work closely with curators and exhibit curators in trying to make the exhibits look as much as possible like the natural environment of the animals. Horticulturists must know which plants will grow well in which exhibits. They must make sure the exhibits do not have plants that the animals will want to eat or that might be poisonous to the animals.

GENERAL CURATOR

General curators make the arrangements for bringing new animals to the zoo. If, for example, a curator wants a new snake or a monkey, he or she will ask the general curator to get one. The general curator will either buy the animal from an animal dealer or another zoo or find it in the wild.

Some curators have the job of keeping records of all the zoo animals. In the records, they list when and where the animals were born and who their parents were.

General curators also help to decide if the zoo should have new exhibits. In this picture the general curator is checking the plans for a new exhibit — a pond for prairie birds.

ANIMAL COMMISSARY KEEPER

Animal commissary keepers order the food that the zoo animals eat. When the food arrives at the zoo, the commissary keepers store it. Some kinds of food must go into freezers or refrigerators. Other food must be put in *dry storage*, or in a place where it will be kept dry.

Animal commissary keepers also raise live food. They raise crickets, flies, worms, and special kinds of grasses. Animal commissary keepers give the live food to the zoo keepers to feed to the birds, snakes, and other zoo animals.

The animal commissary keeper in the picture is working in the room where crickets are raised.

ENGINEER

Engineers keep the zoo's buildings heated and cooled. They also make sure the zoo's electrical system is working right. Engineers repair buildings and build new ones. Mowing the zoo's lawns is another job that engineers do.

Engineers also manage the zoo's water system. They have to make sure all of the water in the zoo is clean and contains the right chemicals. Engineers also make sure the sea animals have the right amount of water to live in and that the water is not too warm or too cold.

Salt is one of the chemicals in the water of the whale's tank. The engineer in the picture is checking the salt content of the water. The water in the tank should be as much as possible like the water the whale lived in when it swam in the ocean.

INTERPRETIVE NATURALIST

Interpretive naturalists take visitors around the zoo. They have learned a lot about animals, so they are able to tell visitors interesting stories about them. Interpretive naturalists also point out animals that visitors might miss, such as an owl perched in a tree or a raccoon hiding in the grass.

In this picture, the interpretive naturalist is standing by a *monorail*, a train that runs on one rail instead of on two. This interpretive naturalist takes visitors around the zoo on the monorail. Very few zoos today have monorails, but many zoos have small trains or buses for visitors to ride.

COORDINATOR OF VOLUNTEER PROGRAMS

The coordinator of volunteer programs recruits the volunteers who help at the zoo. Volunteers are unpaid part-time workers who show visitors around the zoo and answer their questions. Coordinators instruct the volunteers so they will be able to answer the questions of the visitors who come to the zoo.

Coordinators also set up special projects and activities for zoo visitors. If a group of senior citizens were to come to the zoo, for example, a coordinator might have a volunteer demonstrate how zoo keepers handle snakes.

In this picture, the coordinator is discussing with three volunteers information they will share with visitors.

Likes and Dislikes

onkeys choose companions, preferring
some troop members over others.
These relationships are complex,
variable, personalized and rapidly
changing. They can't always be
predicted by rank and role.
Male - female sexual bonds are brief,
lasting only a few days. The female
makes the choice independent of rank.

Can You
Leade

A troop is orga
strict dominance
which maintains order
and preserves t

Each m
in the
(vo

GRAPHIC ARTS SPECIALIST

Graphic arts specialists prepare pictures of the zoo animals for magazines, newspapers, and brochures. The pictures also appear on signs at the zoo. Sign pictures of animals help visitors to recognize the animals they see in the exhibits.

Graphic arts specialists have many different ways of making pictures of animals. They can draw them, paint them, or photograph them. This graphic arts specialist is drawing a picture of a bird. Doesn't the picture of the snake she has drawn look like a real snake?

EDUCATION DIRECTOR

Has anyone ever come to your school to talk about the zoo? That person might have been the zoo's education director. Education directors visit schools to tell students about the zoo. They also talk to school groups that visit the zoo.

Education directors write booklets about the zoo for teachers to use in the classroom. Directors know that people who read and learn more about the zoo will enjoy their visits more.

Some education directors also write zoo newsletters. Newsletters announce special happenings at the zoo such as the birth of a baby animal or the opening of a new exhibit. Education directors want people in the community to know what's new at the zoo.

ZOO STORES SUPERVISOR

Many people who come to the zoo like to go home with souvenirs to remember their visits. Supervisors have charge of the zoo's souvenir stores. Supervisors decide what kind of souvenirs to buy for the stores. Tee-shirts, posters, pictures, and models of animals are a few of the souvenirs that the zoo stores may sell. But the zoo stores sell more than souvenirs. They also sell camera film and refreshments such as soft drinks, candy, and ice cream.

Store supervisors buy everything the stores sell. They learn which souvenirs visitors like to buy and make sure the stores do not run out of the souvenirs that are favorites with visitors.

DIRECTOR OF VISITOR PROGRAMS

Directors of visitor programs have charge of all of the people who provide services to zoo visitors. Directors make sure the interpretive naturalists, store workers, volunteers, and graphic arts specialists are all doing their jobs right. They will also decide how much money these people will be able to spend for their activities.

Directors of visitor programs also think of new programs the zoo can offer visitors, and they *evaluate*, or check, visitor programs to see how successful they are. If a program is not successful, directors will suggest ways to improve it.

The director in the picture is sharing her ideas with the people who will write the training booklets for the zoo's volunteers.

ZOO DIRECTOR

Zoo directors are in charge of the entire zoo. They make the big decisions at the zoo and decide, for example, whether the zoo should *expand*, or grow, or should add more animals. Zoo directors also decide when the zoo should open and close and how much should be charged for admission.

Zoo directors also hire many of the people who help to carry out the important decisions at the zoo. They try to make sure these people do a good job because they want the zoo to be a pleasant place for both animals and visitors.

Zoo directors must also raise money for the zoo, and they often speak to groups about the zoo. They want everyone to know how important the zoo is to the whole community.

PROPOSED BY GOVERNOR ALBERT ROYCE
TO THE SEVENTY-FIRST LEGISLATURE

1979-81

DETAILED BIENNIAL BUDGET PROPOSAL

Zoo careers described in this book

Zoo Keeper

Curator

Exhibit Curator

Veterinarian

Horticulturist

General Curator

Animal Commissary Keeper

Engineer

Interpretive Naturalist

Coordinator of Volunteer Programs

Graphic Arts Specialist

Education Director

Zoo Stores Supervisor

Director of Visitor Programs

Zoo Director

A letter from a zoo director

ZOO
MINNESOTA ZOOLOGICAL GARDEN

12101 Johnny Cake Ridge Road
Apple Valley, MN 55124

Dear Readers,

In this book you have discovered that it takes many people of different talents to run a zoo.

Zoos used to be just a fun place to look at animals. The zoo of today is more of a cross between Noah's Ark and a space ship. The animals must be nourished and protected from extinction for a long journey of many generations. In many cases, there is no wilderness for them to return to. The people must be educated about the needs of the animals while having a delightful time visiting the zoo with their whole families.

I hope that when you now visit your zoo, you will better understand all the different types of work that make today's "Noah's Ark" a success.

Sincerely,

Edward Kohn
General Director

The publisher would like to thank the Minnesota Zoological
Garden for its cooperation in the preparation of this book.

The photographs in this book realistically depict existing
conditions in the service or industry discussed, including the
number of women and minority groups currently employed.

We specialize in publishing quality books for
young people. For a complete list please write

LERNER PUBLICATIONS COMPANY
241 First Avenue North, Minneapolis, Minnesota 55401